The Playground Problem

For the real Emma—M. M.

ISBN 0-439-68081-6

Text copyright © 2004 by Simon & Schuster, Inc. Illustrations copyright © 2004 by Mike Gordon. All rights reserved. Published by Scholastic Inc., 557 Broadway, New York, NY 10012, by arrangement with Aladdin Paperbacks, Simon & Schuster Children's Publishing Division. SCHOLASTIC and associated logos are trademarks and/or registered trademarks of Scholastic Inc.

12 11 10 9 8 7 6 5 4 3 2 1   4 5 6 7 8 9/0

Printed in the U.S.A.   23

First Scholastic printing, September 2004

Book design by Sammy Yuen Jr.

The text of this book was set in Century Schoolbook.

The Playground Problem

Written by Margaret McNamara
Illustrated by Mike Gordon

SCHOLASTIC INC.
New York   Toronto   London   Auckland   Sydney
Mexico City   New Delhi   Hong Kong   Buenos Aires

Monday was a sunny day.

It was recess.
Mrs. Connor's first-grade
class was on
the playground.

The boys were playing soccer.

"Hey!" called Emma.

"May I play?"

"No," said Nick.

"No," said Jamie.

"No," said Reza.

"We do not want you
to play with us,"
said Nick.

"Why not?" asked Emma.
"Because you are a girl,"
said Reza. "And girls
do not play soccer."

Emma was mad.

Emma was
very mad.

Emma was
FURIOUS.

That night she told her dad
all about the boys.

He helped her
figure out a plan.

On Tuesday
the girls ran out
to the playground.

They had a soccer ball.
They played soccer.

"Hey!" said Reza.

"The girls can play soccer."

"They are pretty good,"
said Nick.

"They are very good,"
said Jamie. "Emma! Come
and join the boys' team."

"No," said Emma.

"I do not want to play

on a team with just boys."

"Why not?" asked Nick.

"Figure it out," said Emma.

On Wednesday
it rained and rained.

The girls played
at the activity table.

The boys sat
and stared at the rain.

"What are they doing?"
asked Katie.
"They are figuring
it out," said Emma.

On Thursday
it was sunny again.
The girls were
scoring goals.

"Hey, Emma!" said Reza.
"We figured it out."

"Boys and girls
can play together,"
said Jamie.

"They can play
on the same team,"
said Reza.

"We got it," said Nick.

From then on,
the boys and girls played
together.

Sometimes they played
really well together.

Sometimes they had fights.

"I figure that
playing together makes us
the best team
we can be," said Reza.

And he was right.